To Kari 3rd Birt
From Great Mama

THE TALKING MICKEY MOUSE SHOW™

The Impossible Journey

Printed in Hong Kong. /D83 ISBN: 1-55578-300-7
12345 7890

Mickey One of our most exciting trips started the day Goofy helped me build a doghouse for Pluto. I guess you could say it started off with a bang.

Goofy Yeow, my thumb!

Mickey Be careful with that hammer, Goofy. We're almost done.

Goofy If I keep this up, my hand will be almost done!

Mickey You know, Goofy, I have the strangest feeling we forgot something.

Goofy Yeah, a first aid kit!

Mickey No, I mean part of the doghouse. Oh well, I guess I'm just imagining things.

Goofy	Well, I guess that just leaves the roof.
Mickey	Okay, Goofy, step inside the doghouse. I'll hand you the roof.
Goofy	Got it, Mick. I'll hold it from in here while you nail it shut. There, I guess that about does it. Looks good from in here. 'Course, it's kinda dark.
Mickey	Goofy, I think I know what we forgot.
Goofy	What's that, Mick?
Mickey	A door.

Mickey	With a saw, I cut a door in the front of the doghouse. But before Goofy could come out, Pluto went in!
Goofy	Good dog! Down, Pluto, down! Yeow!
Mickey	Pretty soon, all that was left of the doghouse was a pile of boards. Pluto sat in the middle, licking Goofy's face.

Mickey Just then I heard a voice behind me. It was our mailman, Donald Duck.

Donald Oh, hello, Mickey. Here's a package for you.

Goofy Hey, Pluto, don't bark at Donald. He's our friend.

Mickey Down, Pluto, down!

Donald Mickey, you should do something about that dog of yours. Say, why don't you use this pile of boards to build him a doghouse?

Mickey A doghouse! Gee, thanks for the idea.

Donald You're welcome, Mickey. See you tomorrow.

Goofy Say, Mick, what's this package he left?

Mickey It's from Dr. Stan Livingstone, and it came all the way from Africa!

Goofy Africa? Wow, that's pretty far away, isn't it, Mick?

Mickey It sure is, Goofy—thousands of miles.

Goofy Look, there's a tag on the package.

Mickey It says not to open except in an emergency. I guess we'd better do as it says.

Mickey I wrote a letter to Stan to tell him we'd received his package. Then Goofy and I headed for the post office to mail it.

Goofy Say, Mick, who's this Dr. Livingstone?

Mickey Stan's the world's greatest explorer. He's in Africa looking for the legendary Bottomless Lake. For years people have been searching for it . . . but none of them ever returned!

Goofy Hey Mick, look who's standing in front of the post office—Minnie Mouse!

Mickey Hello, Minnie. Gee, you look pretty today.

Minnie Hi, Mickey. Hi, Goofy. What brings you to town?

Goofy We're mailing a letter to Dr. Stan Livingstone. You know, the famous explorer.

Minnie But Goofy, didn't you hear? Stan Livingstone was reported missing. It's been in all the papers. They're saying it may be *impossible* to find him.

Mickey Gee, thanks for telling us, Minnie. I guess this letter won't do any good now. Come on, Goofy, let's go back to my house. This is an emergency.

Goofy Emergency! That means we can open the package.

Goofy When we got home, Mickey tore open the package. There was a note inside from Stan Livingstone.

Mickey "Dear Mickey: This package contains five impossible berries, found only at the bottom of the Bottomless Lake. Once every hundred years, a few berries float to the surface. That's where I found these."

Goofy Gawrsh, Mick, he found the Bottomless Lake!

Mickey There's more, Goofy. Listen: "Guard these berries carefully, because when eaten they give you the power to do the impossible. Signed, Stan Livingstone."

Goofy Gawrsh, this Stan Livingstone must be quite a feller!

Mickey He sure is, Goofy, and I'll bet he's at the Bottomless Lake right now. If these berries really work, maybe we could use them to find Stan!

Mickey	Goofy ran outside and pointed at the sky.
Goofy	Why don't we try hitching a ride on an airplane?
Mickey	Oh, Goofy, that's impossible. Impossible! If I eat an impossible berry, maybe we can do it!
Goofy	Okay, Mick, down the hatch! Look, there's a plane. Hold out your thumb!
Mickey	Gee, Goofy, I feel kind of silly.
Goofy	Mickey, it's landing! And the pilot's waving to us!
Pilot	Where are you fellows headed? I'm on my way to Africa.
Goofy	Gawrsh, mister, so are we! Thanks.

Mickey We were over the ocean in no time. But the pilot didn't look too happy.

Pilot Uh-oh, black clouds. Sorry, but my plane's too small to handle a storm that big. We'll have to turn back.

Goofy But mister, can't we just fly over the clouds?

Pilot Impossible! This plane could never fly that high.

Goofy Impossible? Well, Mick, try another berry!

Mickey Okay, Goofy, here goes!

Pilot Holy smoke, we're at 25,000 feet and still climbing. I don't know what you fellows did, but it sure worked!

Mickey A few hours later we landed. We were in Africa! I bought some supplies, and Goofy went off to hire a guide. When he came back, he was as pale as a ghost.

Goofy No one wants to go near the Bottomless Lake. They say there's a m-m-monster there!

Mickey Oh Goofy, don't be silly. That's just a superstition.

Goofy But how do we know for sure? Maybe they know something we don't.

Mickey All I know is that there's no such thing as a monster. Now come on, we'll go by ourselves. Stan Livingstone needs our help!

Goofy Okay, Mick. But no explorer has ever returned from the Bottomless Lake.

Mickey But none of them had impossible berries to help them. Just think, we could be the first, if we're careful.

Mickey	Pretty soon we'd left the town behind, and Goofy and I were on our own.
Goofy	Well, I guess this is what they call the jungle. You don't think there are any lions or tigers around here, do you?
Mickey	What's wrong, Goofy? Afraid of hunting wild animals?
Goofy	Gawrsh, no. It's finding 'em that worries me!

Mickey For the rest of the day we kept looking for signs of Stan Livingstone, but we didn't find anything. Then late in the afternoon, Goofy stopped suddenly.

Goofy We're getting near some water, Mick. I can tell by the way my big toe's throbbing.

Mickey Hm, it says on the map here it's the Mumbo Jumbo River.

Goofy Great! Let's go for a swim! Have you ever seen my super duper swan dive?

Mickey No, but I have a feeling I'm going to now.

Goofy That's right, Mick. Here I go!

Mickey Wait a minute, what are those eyes sticking out of the water? Goofy, look out! Crocodiles!

Goofy Yeow! You know, Mick, maybe I'm not in the mood to go swimming after all.

Mickey But how are we going to get across?

Goofy Looks impossible. Hold on a minute! Did I say impossible? Bring out those berries!

Mickey I ate another berry. Then we moved into the water, one step at a time.

Goofy Well, can you beat that! The crocodiles are acting as gentle as little puppy dogs. Hey, I think I'll try something. Watch this, Mick!

Mickey How did you do that? You're riding that crocodile just like a horse!

Goofy Go ahead and try it, Mick. They won't hurt you.

Mickey Hey, this is fun!

Goofy Whoa! Ride 'em, cowboy!

Goofy Gawrsh, that was some ride. But look—what's that hanging from the tree limb?

Mickey It's Stan's hat! And look—here are some footprints!

Goofy They lead through these trees right to this lion. Lion? Run for it, Mick!

Mickey We can't go faster than a lion, Goofy. That's impossible!

Goofy Then you'd better eat another berry—and hurry!

Mickey	I just swallowed one, Goofy. But the lion's not stopping. He's coming right at me!
Goofy	Duck, Mickey, duck!
Mickey	I can't, Goofy. I'm too s-s-scared.
Goofy	Well, what do you know—that lion jumped over your head and banged his head against a tree. He's out cold!
Mickey	See, Goofy? There was really nothing to it.

Goofy Look, Mick, here are Stan's footprints again! They go to this cliff, but then they stop. I guess we've lost his trail.

Mickey Then we're lost, too. I guess if you're not the world's greatest explorer, finding the Bottomless Lake really is impossible.

Goofy Impossible? Maybe it's time for another berry, Mick.

Mickey But it's the last one! Oh well, we've got to find Stan. Here goes!

Goofy Look, Mick, over behind those trees. I see water! This must be it—the Bottomless Lake!

Mickey And here are some more of Stan's footprints. They lead right into the water—but they don't come back out!

Goofy Poor guy. The monster must have got him!

Mickey For the last time, Goofy, there *is* no monster! Now come on, it's getting dark. Let's turn in for the night, and tomorrow we'll try to find Stan.

Mickey	It must have been around four in the morning when I heard a noise. I asked Goofy if he'd heard it, too.
Goofy	I sure did, Mick. It's my teeth rattling.
Mickey	No, I'm talking about that other noise—the wet, sloshy sound. Hear it? It sounds like something that just came out of the water and is standing right . . . over . . . us.
Goofy	Oh, please, Mr. Monster, don't hurt us. Oh, where are our berries now that we need them?

Mickey That's when it hit me. I climbed out of my sleeping bag, walked right up to the monster, and said, "Dr. Livingstone, I presume."

Stan Mickey? Mickey Mouse? Thank goodness you've come!

Goofy Hold on, Mick. You mean the monster's named Dr. Livingstone, too?

Mickey No, Goofy, there's no such thing as a monster. And since only one person before us has ever made it to the Bottomless Lake, I knew this 'monster' had to be Stan.

Goofy Well, I'll be. How'd you walk underwater, Doc?

Stan By eating an impossible berry! I used one to go to the bottom of the lake and back to look for some more berries.

Mickey What took you so long?

Goofy Yeah, all the papers said you were missing for weeks.

Stan It's a long trip. After all, the lake is bottomless! Unfortunately, it's also berry-less. Thank heavens we still have the ones I sent you.

Mickey We've got some bad news for you, Stan. We used up all the berries finding you.

Mickey	For a minute it looked like he was mad. Then he got a sad little smile on his face and sighed.
Stan	Well, I don't suppose I can get angry about two friends trying to help me. Come on, gentlemen, the sun will be coming up soon. Let's start back. I have a feeling you'll be getting a hero's welcome for rescuing me.
Goofy	You know, Mick, things sure turn out funny sometimes.
Mickey	How's that, Goofy?
Goofy	Well, I was thinking—today I'm a hero, and just yesterday I was in the doghouse!